poems compiled by Nancy Larrick
art by Ed Young

Philomel Books   New York

Mice Are Nice

Original text copyright © 1990 by Nancy Larrick.
Illustrations copyright © 1990 by Ed Young.
Published by Philomel Books,
a division of The Putnam & Grosset Group,
200 Madison Avenue, New York, NY 10016.
All rights reserved. Published simultaneously in Canada.
Printed in Hong Kong by South China Printing Co. (1988) Ltd.
The text is set in Veljovic Book.

Library of Congress Cataloging-in-Publication Data
Mice are nice, compiled by Nancy Larrick: illustrated by Ed Young. p. cm.
Includes indexes.
Summary: A collection of poems about mice by A. A. Milne,
John Ciardi, Ian Serraillier, and others.
  1. Mice—Juvenile poetry. 2. Children's poetry.
[1. Mice—Poetry. 2. Poetry—Collections] I. Larrick,
Nancy. II. Young, Ed, ill.
PN6110.M43M54   1988   808.81'936   87-11159
ISBN 0-399-21495-X

First Impression

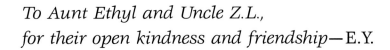

To Aunt Ethyl and Uncle Z.L.,
for their open kindness and friendship—E.Y.

For those who cherish the littlest ones—N.L.

Contents

Mice Are Nice

We heard a tiny twittering. There he was again . . . looking down on us from his wee hole alongside rough stones of the cabin chimney. A deer mouse! *Our* deer mouse, as we had come to say. Beady eyes sparkled in a tiny face caught between bat ears a size too big.

For the past week he had come each evening to people-watch. And we watched back as though expecting a friendly conversation to open up between us.

It never did, of course, but I found myself drawn deeper and deeper into the personality behind those twinkling eyes and wide pearl-gray ears. Now I was beginning to see why poets, storytellers and artists around the world have so often directed their talents toward the mouse.

In Japan the white mouse is believed to bring good luck, and the Japanese calendar of years begins with the Year of the Mouse. It is not surprising, then, that one of the earliest Japanese children's books is *The Wedding of the Mouse,* painted in exquisite pictures on a long scroll. Another of that same period is *The Tale of the Mouse.*

In the Western world as well, children meet charming and irresistible mice in their picture books and stories: Mrs. Tittlemouse, created by Beatrix Potter; the Dormouse in *Alice in Wonderland;* Stewart Little from E. B. White; Papa Mouse and the seven mouse boys by Arnold Lobel . . . even "Three Blind Mice," which is probably the best-known round in the English language. Poets too have been caught up in the charm of mice.

Mice Are Nice brings together some of the choicest poems about mice—city mice and country mice, spinning mice and runaway mice, a mouse in a rocket, even a light-house-keeper's white-mouse!

Nancy Larrick

Message from a Mouse, Ascending in a Rocket

Attention, architect!
Attention, engineer!
A message from mouse
Coming clear:

"Suggest installing
Spike or sprocket
Easily turned by
A mouse in a rocket;
An ejection gadget
Simple to handle
To free mouse quickly
From this space-age ramble.
Suggest packing
For the next moon trip
A mouse-sized parachute
Somewhere in the ship,
So I can descend
(When my fear comes strong)
Back to earth where I was born.
Back to the cheerful world of cheese
        And small mice playing,
        And my wife waiting."

                    Patricia Hubbell

The City Mouse and the Garden Mouse

The city mouse lives in a house;
    The garden mouse lives in a bower,
He's friendly with the frogs and toads,
    And sees the pretty plants in flower.

The city mouse eats bread and cheese;
    The garden mouse eats what he can;
We will not grudge him seeds and stalks,
    Poor little, timid, furry man.

Christina Georgina Rossetti

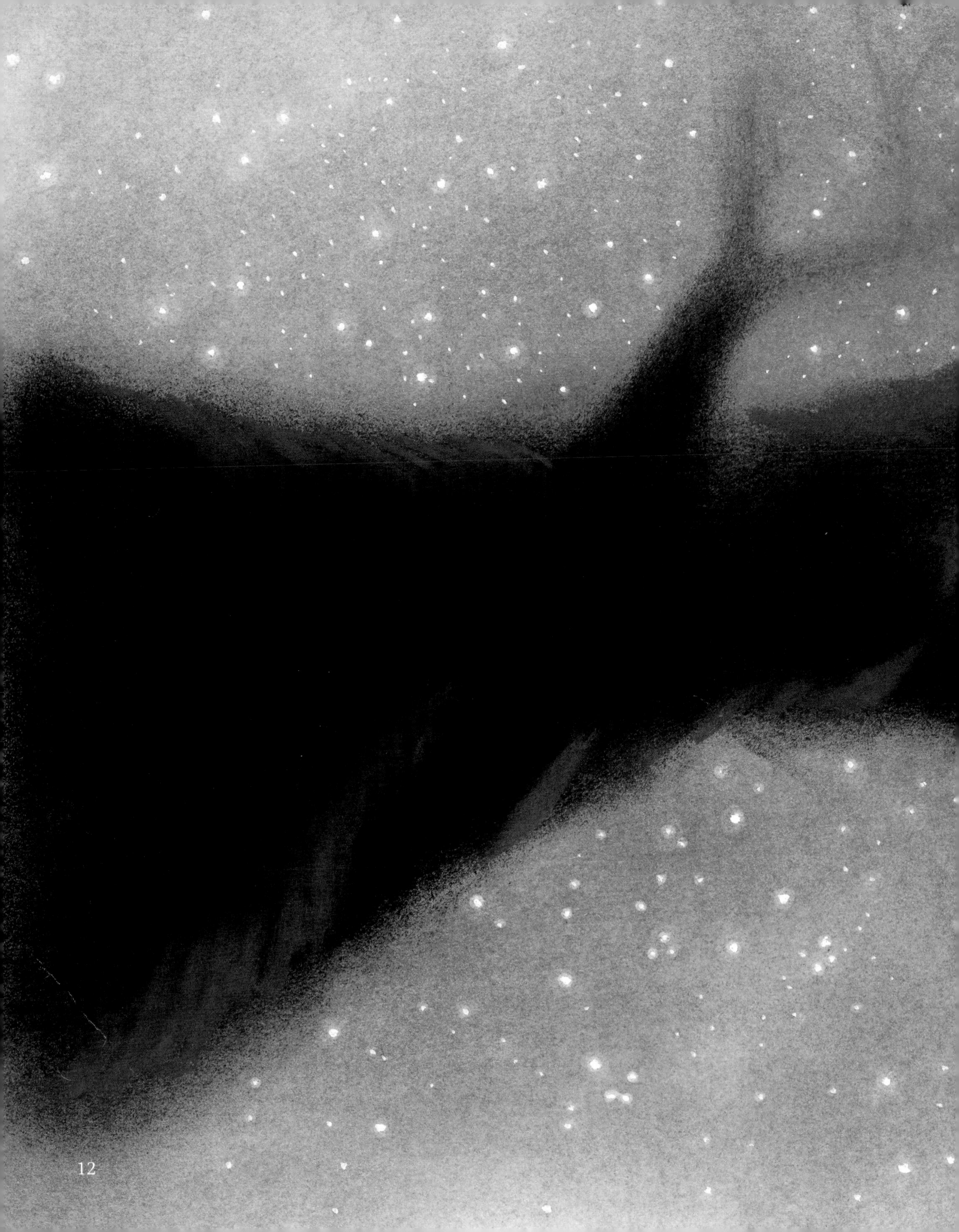

In the Dark of Night

A mouse goes out
in the dark of night
without a lantern
or other light.
She's not afraid
of the dark at all,
though the night's so big
and herself so small.

Aileen Fisher

Anybody Home?

I'd like to look
in a meadowy nook
at the small grass house
of a mother mouse
in a velvety blouse.

I'd like to peek
in the door and see
six pink babies
who couldn't see me.

Aileen Fisher

David's Mouse

Twiverey Twinkeley, my white mouse,
Lives in a box inside my house,
Twiverey Twinkeley, his pink nose,
Quivers and quavers wherever he goes;
Twiverey Twinkeley, his bright eyes,
Blink at me like quick pink flies,
　　Down he leaps to sleep to sleep
　Shredded paper in a heap
　　Up he pops and winks his eyes
　To view a mouse's paradise
　　Corn in corners
　　Candy wrappers
　　Shredded paper
　　Cloth in tatters
　　Bits of cheeses
　　　Piled high
　And oh! the light
　In Twinkle's eye.

Patricia Hubbell

The Light-House-Keeper's White-Mouse

As I rowed out to the light-house
For a cup of tea one day,
I came on a very wet white-mouse
Out swimming in the bay.

"If you are for the light-house,"
Said he, "I'm glad we met.
I'm the light-house-keeper's white-mouse
And I fear I'm getting wet."

"O light-house-keeper's white-mouse,
I am rowing out for tea
With the keeper in his light-house.
Let me pull you in with me."

So I gave an oar to the white-mouse.
And I pulled on the other.
And we all had tea at the light-house
With the keeper and his mother.

John Ciardi

The House of the Mouse

The house of the mouse
is a wee little house,
a green little house in the grass,
which big clumsy folk
may hunt and may poke
and still never see as they pass
this sweet little, neat little,
wee little, green little,
cuddle-down hide-away
house in the grass.

Lucy Sprague Mitchell

The Meadow Mouse

1

In a shoe box stuffed in an old nylon stocking
Sleeps the baby mouse I found in the meadow,
Where he trembled and shook beneath a stick
Till I caught him by the tail and brought him in,
Cradled in my hand.
A little quaker, the whole body of him trembling,
His absurd whiskers sticking out like a cartoon-mouse,
His feet like small leaves,
Little lizard-feet,
Whitish and spread wide when he tried to struggle away,
Wriggling like a minuscule puppy.

Now he's eaten three kinds of cheese and drunk from his bottle-cap watering-trough—
So much he just lies in one corner,
His tail curled under him, his belly big
As his head; his bat-like ears
Twitching, tilting toward the least sound.

Do I imagine he no longer trembles
When I come close to him?
He seems no longer to tremble.

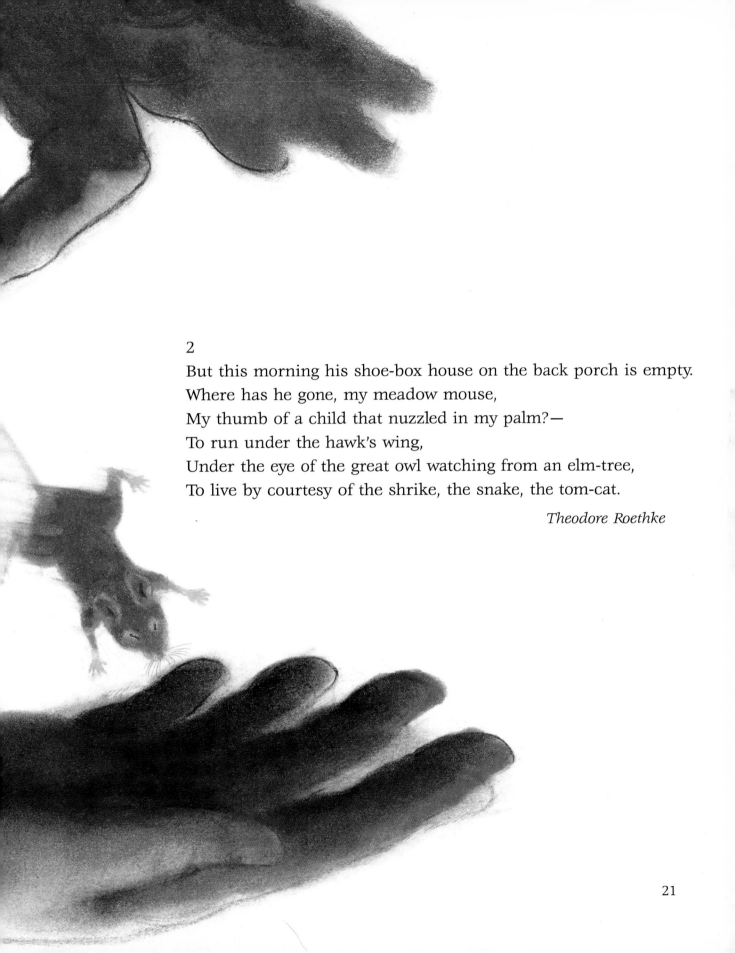

2
But this morning his shoe-box house on the back porch is empty.
Where has he gone, my meadow mouse,
My thumb of a child that nuzzled in my palm?—
To run under the hawk's wing,
Under the eye of the great owl watching from an elm-tree,
To live by courtesy of the shrike, the snake, the tom-cat.

Theodore Roethke

A Friendly Mouse

The sun was leaning across the ground
When I heard a tiny twittering sound.
And a mouse who didn't seem to be
A bit afraid came close to me.

He sat up and nibbled a leaf of clover
And twinkled his nose and looked me over.
I held out my hand to coax him near.
He washed his whiskers, he washed one ear.

Then suddenly he wasn't there
On the ground in the grass but up in my hair!
I carefully walked into our house
And told my mother I'd caught a mouse.

That's nice dear, she said. Then she saw it was true
And stared like she didn't know what to do
Except to remember that one of her joys
Is to show an interest in what interests boys.

She tried to, but couldn't. She glared at my mouse
And said, *Get that creature out of this house!*
I did. He squeaked a small squeak to say
He understood. Then he ran away.

Harry Behn

23

The Mouse

I heard a mouse
Bitterly complaining
In a crack of moonlight
Aslant on the floor—

"Little I ask
And that little is not granted;
There are few crumbs
In this world any more.

"The bread box is tin
And I cannot get in.

"The jam's in a jar
My teeth cannot mar.

"The cheese sits by itself
On an ice-box shelf.

"All night I run
Searching and seeking;
All night I run
About on the floor.

"Moonlight is there
And a bare place for dancing,
But no little feast
Is spread anymore."

Elizabeth Coatsworth

Mice

I think mice
Are rather nice

Their tails are long,
Their faces small,
They haven't any
Chins at all.
Their ears are pink,
Their teeth are white,
They run about
The house at night.
They nibble things
They shouldn't touch
And no one seems
to like them much.

But I think mice
Are nice.

Rose Fyleman

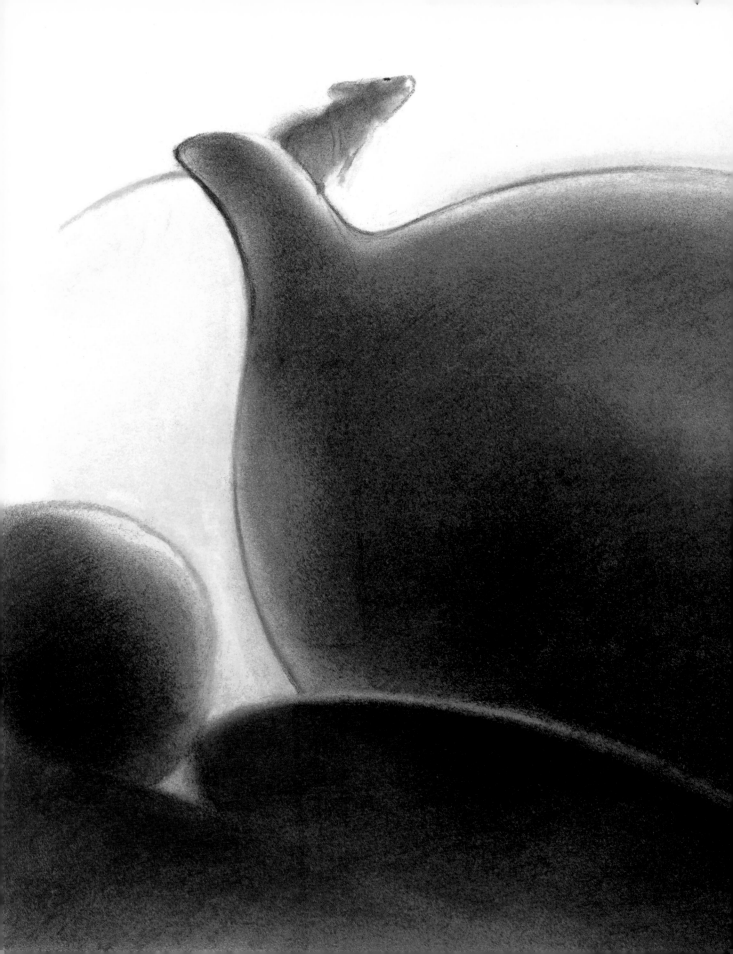

Calico Pie

Calico Ban
The little Mice ran,
To be ready in time for tea,
Flippity flup,
They drank it all up,
And danced in the cup,—
But they never came back to me!
They never came back!
They never came back!
They never came back to me!

Edward Lear

The Cat Who Aspired to Higher Things

Our cat turns up her nose at mice.
She thinks rhinoceroses
Are twice as nice as mice to chase,
But now the mice are everyplace,

In the furnace,
In the freezer,
In Aunt Edith's orange squeezer,

In the cellar,
In the cider,
In Great-Grandpa's best hang-glider,

In the ginger,
In the allspice,
In Aunt Flora's King Kong false face,

In the stamps,
In the chocolate section
Of my ice cream cone collection—

X. J. Kennedy

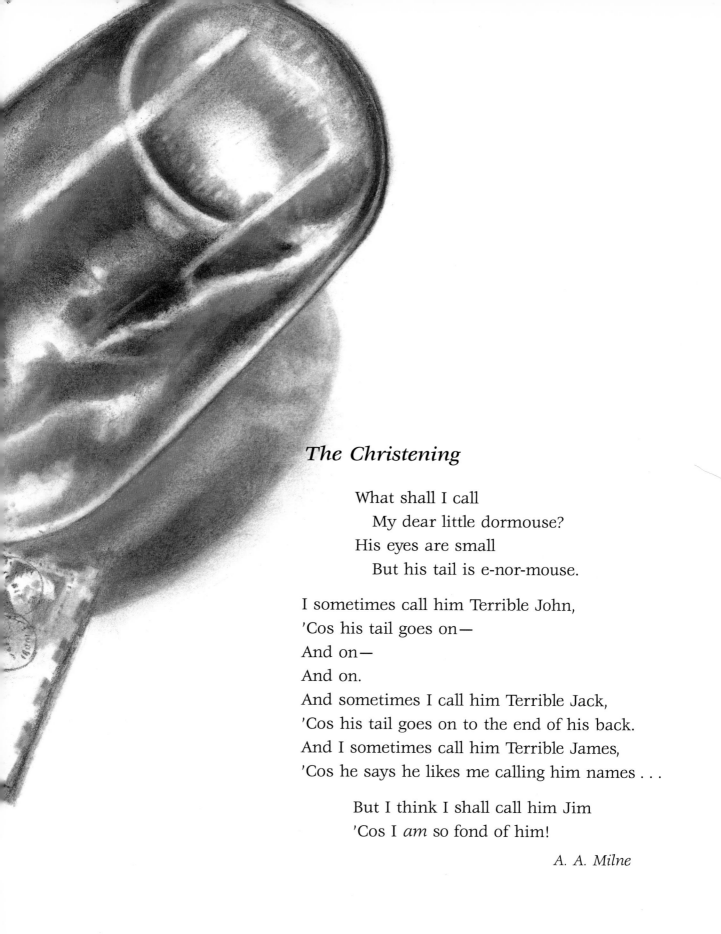

The Christening

What shall I call
    My dear little dormouse?
His eyes are small
    But his tail is e-nor-mouse.

I sometimes call him Terrible John,
'Cos his tail goes on—
And on—
And on.
And sometimes I call him Terrible Jack,
'Cos his tail goes on to the end of his back.
And I sometimes call him Terrible James,
'Cos he says he likes me calling him names . . .

But I think I shall call him Jim
'Cos I *am* so fond of him!

A. A. Milne

The House Mouse

Little brown house mouse, laugh and leap,
chitter and cheep while the cat's asleep,
chatter and call and slip through the wall,
trip through the kitchen, skip through the hall.

Little brown house mouse, don't be meek,
dance and squeak and prance and tweak.
There's cheese to take and plenty of cake
so long as you're gone when the cat's awake.

Jack Prelutsky

26 ¢
PLAZAS

BURING

Imported Long Filler - Natural Leaf Binder

MADE
FROM Natural TOBACCOS
...TASTE THE DIFFERENCE.

32

Missing

Has anybody seen my mouse?

I opened his box for just a minute,
Just to make sure he was really in it,
And while I was looking, he jumped outside!
I tried to catch him, I tried, I tried. . . .
I think he's somewhere about the house.
Has *anyone* seen my mouse?

Uncle John, have you seen my mouse?

Just a small sort of mouse, a dear little brown one,
He came from the country, he isn't a town one,
So he'll feel all lonely in a London street;
Why, what could he possibly find to eat?

He must be somewhere. I'll ask Aunt Rose:
Have *you* seen a mouse with a woffelly nose?
Oh, somewhere about—
He's just got out. . . .

Hasn't *anybody* seen my mouse?

A. A. Milne

Cat and Mouse Game

Down in the cellar where the green toads hop
Lives a small grey mouse
    in a grey stone house,
In a grey stone house near a dry-laid wall
Where the green toads hop
    on the damp dirt floor;
A small, grey, flicker-whiskered,
    pink-nosed mouse
With a long grey rat-tail curling on the end,
Curling down the stone wall whenever he walks,
Curling down the dry-laid, grey stone wall.

Down in the cellar creeps
    the mouse-furred cat,
Licking-whiskered, mouse-furred,
    full-tailed cat,
Licking at her whiskers with
    a mouse-filled brain
Flexing out her claws, flexing out her claws,
Can I catch him? Can I catch him?
    Can I catch him soon?
Cat lies, tiger-like, stretched full-moon.
Down in the cellar where the green toads hop,
Grey mouse watches from a grey stone wall.
Can I catch him? Can I catch him?
    Can I catch him soon?

Cat lies thinking in a pouncing swoon.
    Stiff-backed
Stiff-pawed, flex-clawed cat
Lies like a panther, waiting to attack.

Grey mouse stiffens, too, never moves an eye,
Never moves an eye, never flicks a whisker,
Lies in the stone-walled, grey foundation.
Cat lies, mouse lies, still as dark,
Down in the cellar where the green toads hop.

Suddenly kitty, with a yawning purr,
Stretches her back like a waking girl,
Stretches her back and moves for the stair,
Heads for the kitchen and laps her milk,
Laps at her milk with a quick pink tongue,
Licks at her whiskers and purrs replete,
"I never did, never did, like mouse meat!"

Patricia Hubbell

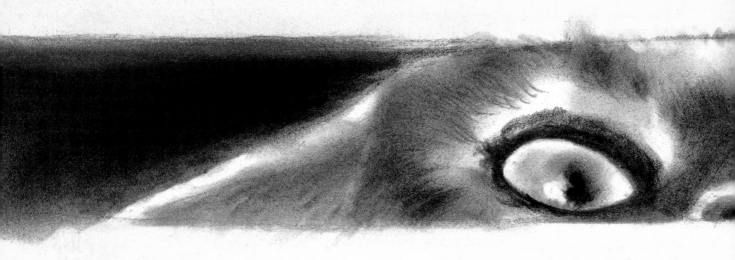

Six Little Mice

Six little mice sat down to spin;
Pussy passed by and she peeped in.
What are you doing, my little men?
Weaving coats for gentlemen.
Shall I come in and cut off your threads?
No, no, Mistress Pussy, you'd bite off our heads.
Oh, no, I'll not; I'll help you to spin.
That may be so, but you don't come in.

From Mother Goose

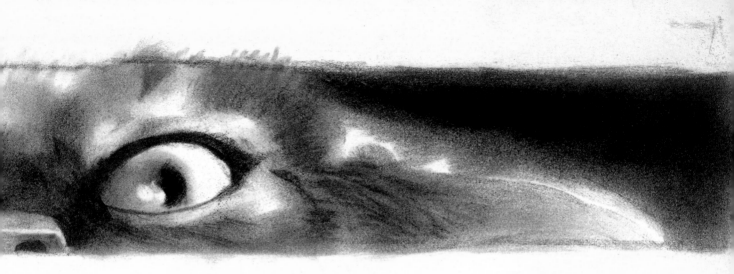

I Wouldn't

There's a mouse house
In the hall wall
With a small door
By the hall floor
Where the fat cat
Sits all day
Sits that way
All day
Every day
Just to say,
"Come out and play"
To the nice mice
In the hall wall
With the small door
By the hall floor.

And do they
Come out and play
When the fat cat
Asks them to?

Well, would you?

John Ciardi

The Prayer of the Mouse

I am so little and grey,
dear God,
How can You keep me in mind?
Always spied upon,
always chased.
Nobody ever gives me anything,
and I nibble meagerly at life.
Why do they reproach me with being a mouse?
Who made me but You?
I only ask to stay hidden.
Given me my hunger's pittance
safe from the claws
of that devil with green eyes.

Carmen Bernos de Gasztold

There Was a Mouse

There was a mouse
who used to sit
about the house
all day and knit
until the cat
got wind of it.
The cat
and all her kittens
came and ate
that mouse's mittens.

Karla Kuskin

Cats and Dogs

Some like cats, and some like dogs,
and both of course are nice
if cats and dogs are what you want
—but I myself like mice.

For dogs chase cats, and cats chase rats
—I guess they think it's fun.
I like my mouse the most because
he won't chase anyone.

N. M. Bodecker

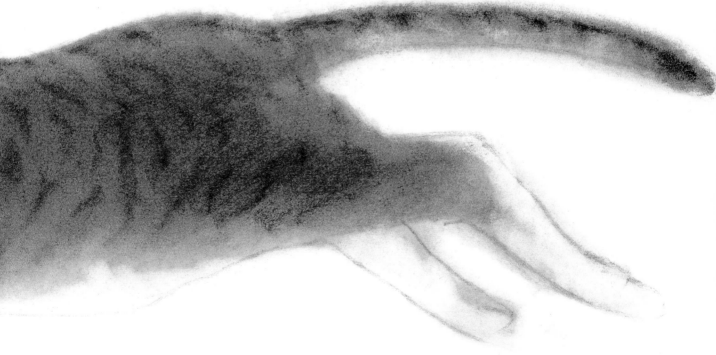

The Mouse in the Wainscot

Hush, Suzanne!
Don't lift your cup.
That breath you heard
Is a mouse getting up.

As the mist that steams
From your milk as you sup,
So soft is the sound
Of a mouse getting up.

There! did you hear
His feet pitter-patter,
Lighter than tipping
Of beads on a platter,

And then like a shower
On the window pane
The little feet scampering
Back again?

O falling of feather!
O drift of leaf!
The mouse in the wainscot
Is dropping asleep.

Ian Serraillier

Wanted

I'm looking for a house
Said the little brown mouse,
    with
One room for breakfast,
One room for tea,
One room for supper,
And that makes three.

One room to dance in,
When I give a ball,
A kitchen and a bedroom,
Six rooms in all.

Rose Fyleman

43

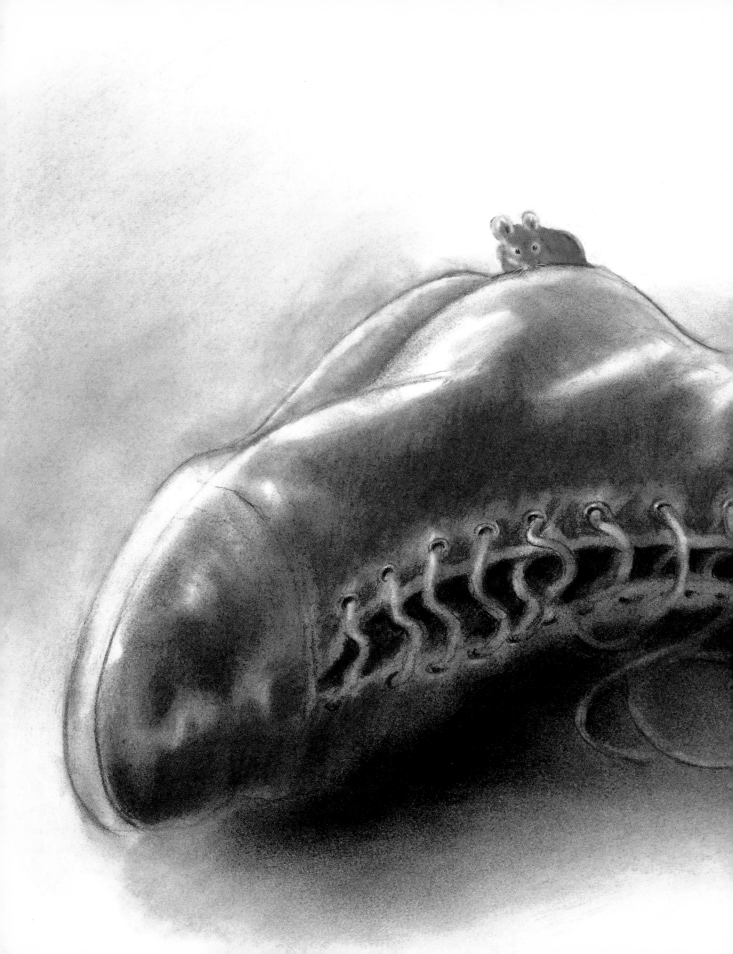

Mice

Mice
Find places
In places,

A dark
Hall behind
The hall,

Odd rooms
That other
Rooms hide:

A world
Inside
The wide world,

And space enough,
Even in
Small spaces.

Valerie Worth

Index of Poets and Poems